7 Days Princess

JULIA WU

Copyright © 2022 Julia Wu.

All rights reserved. No part of this book may be used or reproduced by any means, graphic, electronic, or mechanical, including photocopying, recording, taping or by any information storage retrieval system without the written permission of the author except in the case of brief quotations embodied in critical articles and reviews.

Balboa Press books may be ordered through booksellers or by contacting:

Balboa Press
A Division of Hay House
1663 Liberty Drive
Bloomington, IN 47403
www.balboapress.com.au
AU TFN: 1 800 844 925 (Toll Free inside Australia)
AU Local: 0283 107 086 (+61 2 8310 7086 from outside Australia)

Because of the dynamic nature of the Internet, any web addresses or links contained in this book may have changed since publication and may no longer be valid. The views expressed in this work are solely those of the author and do not necessarily reflect the views of the publisher, and the publisher hereby disclaims any responsibility for them.

Any people depicted in stock imagery provided by Getty Images are models, and such images are being used for illustrative purposes only.
Certain stock imagery © Getty Images.

ISBN: 978-1-9822-9579-0 (sc)
ISBN: 978-1-9822-9580-6 (e)

Print information available on the last page.

Balboa Press rev. date: 10/26/2022

BALBOA.PRESS
A DIVISION OF HAY HOUSE

For my lovely mother and father, family, extended family, Aunty Wong, Uncle Wong, Uncle George, Reverend Wilfred, Friends, and Everyone who are kind, thoughtful, considerate, courteous, understanding and contribute to designing beautiful moments for each other.

There was once a little princess. She lived in Cloud 9, one of the many moons of Jupiter.[1] Every day, she saw Jupiter, like a big brother, furiously trying to protect Earth from all the asteroids shooting towards it. She saw that the sun gave light to Earth, and she was very interested in visiting it.

She came to Earth because of a magical space butterfly. When she was on Earth, she saw that it was perfect. Nature was perfect, and all creatures, including small bees, were supporting the great order of a lively, vibrant, and magnificent ecosystem.

---

[1] As of August 2021, Jupiter has fifty-six named moons and twenty-six awaiting official names (https://solarsystem.nasa.gov/moons/jupiter-moons/overview). Cloud 9 is one of the twenty-six unnamed moons.

CHAPTER 1

The Little Princess's First Day on Land

On the first day on land, she met a lady who lived in a tall skyscraper and came out for a slow stroll using a cane. She was mumbling about unclean water everywhere she has lived, like when she turned on the kitchen tap, the water was always too unclean to drink.

The little princess asked, "Have you seen my Sweetie Pinky?" She described the chicken to the lovely old lady.

Sweetie Pinky was the little princess's pet. She was a silkie bantam chicken who was very fluffy and sweet-looking. Because of the low gravity on Cloud 9, Sweetie Pinky had grown to be the size of a poodle, much larger than the size of a regular silkie bantam on Earth. The migration birds, who frequently visited the little princess's persimmon orchard in Cloud 9, did not close Sweetie Pinky's coop door after visiting her. Because of her curious character, she wandered off into the vast plains in Cloud 9.

The old lady said to the little princess, "You seem stressed looking for your chicken." She then added, "I am 102 years old. I have lived many times your age and have been through many things in life. If you are stressed at such a young age because you cannot find a chicken, I can assure you everything will be fine. You'll be all right. Don't stress while looking for your chicken. If you are stressed, it means you have not encountered such a situation with your current experience." She continued through her journey as if life was passing her by, yet she always had a choice.

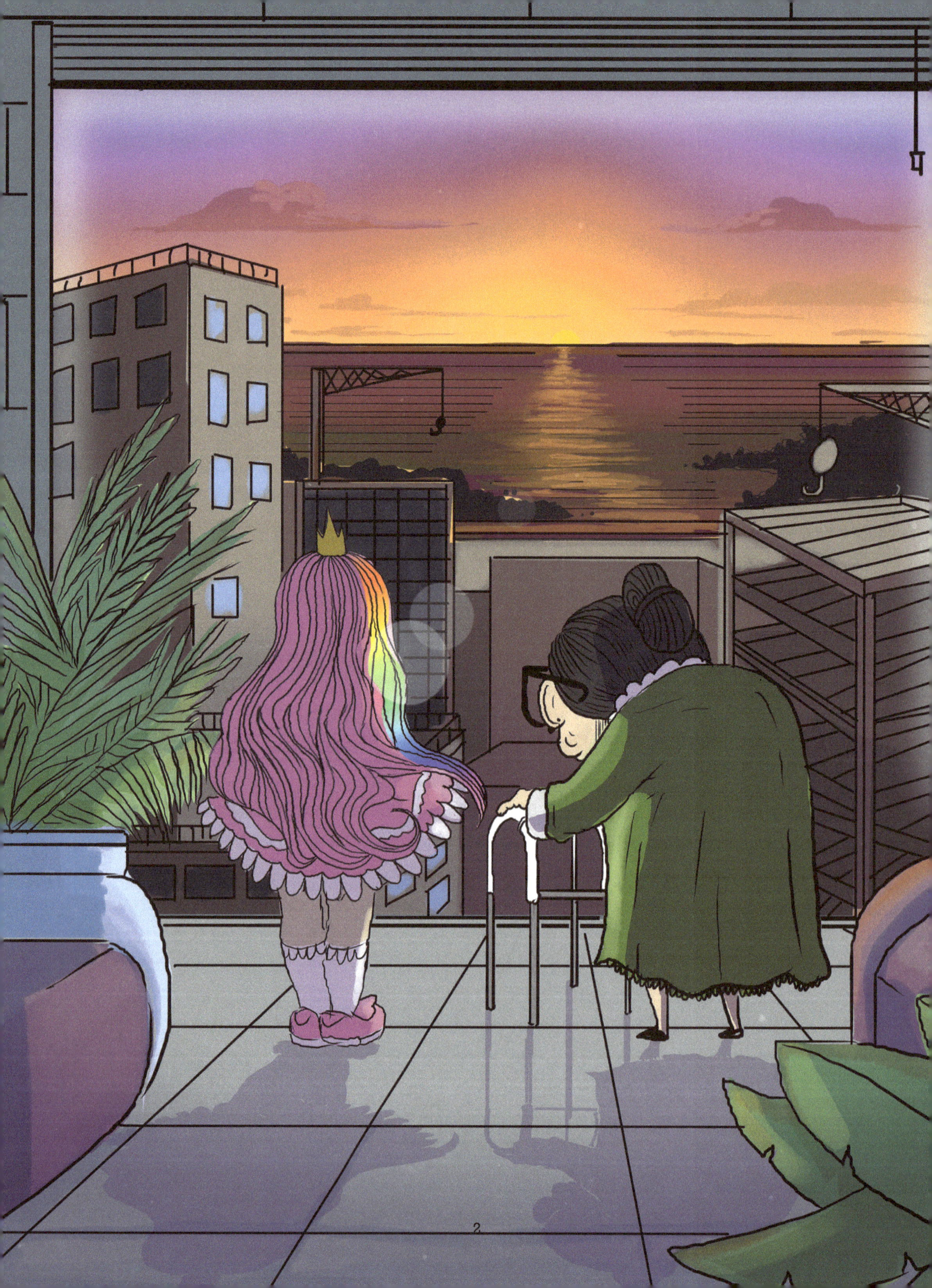

The little princess closed her eyes and breathed in and out four times to calm herself down. She recognised that each journey was a new experience. However, she was well and humbled enough to appreciate the wisdom imparted by the old lady by saying "Thank you".

The little princess did not find the chicken, Sweetie Pinky, on the first day.

CHAPTER 2

The Little Princess's Second Day on Land

On the second day, the magical butterfly dropped her off at another location by the lake. There she found clean water and also met an engineer. She asked the engineer, "Why is there unclean water in one place and clean water in another?"

The engineer responded, "There are many places on land, and each place has people with talent, standards, and style. Some call them society leaders. These leaders are entrusted with bigger responsibilities. They prioritise different visions and missions. Here, we value what cannot be seen, such as the well-working sewage system underground. Where you were previously, they care more about skyscrapers, beauty above land. And it's a choice by the leaders of the day what they would like to prioritise. There is no right or wrong; it is just their preferred style of the day."

5

The little princess did not find the chicken, Sweetie Pinky, by the lake on the second day.

CHAPTER 3

The Little Princess's Third Day on Land

On the third day, the magical space butterfly dropped her by the forest. There, the little princess felt the air was very fresh and the environment very calm. She met an able vagabond. "Life is difficult and lonely here," he said.

She saw a beautiful environment filled with fresh air and plenty of fruitful trees, yet he yearned for more. The vagabond shared his vision of living in grandeur. The little princess was yet to understand grandeur. She saw that his happiness was dependent on his vision and that its lack of fulfilment was weighing on him. He had a heavy workload on his mind and an unfulfilled heart. To the little princess, there seemed nothing more to add or subtract in his world. He had a bed made of fern. The food in his belly was catered by the nearby fruit trees. And the little princess continued her journey.

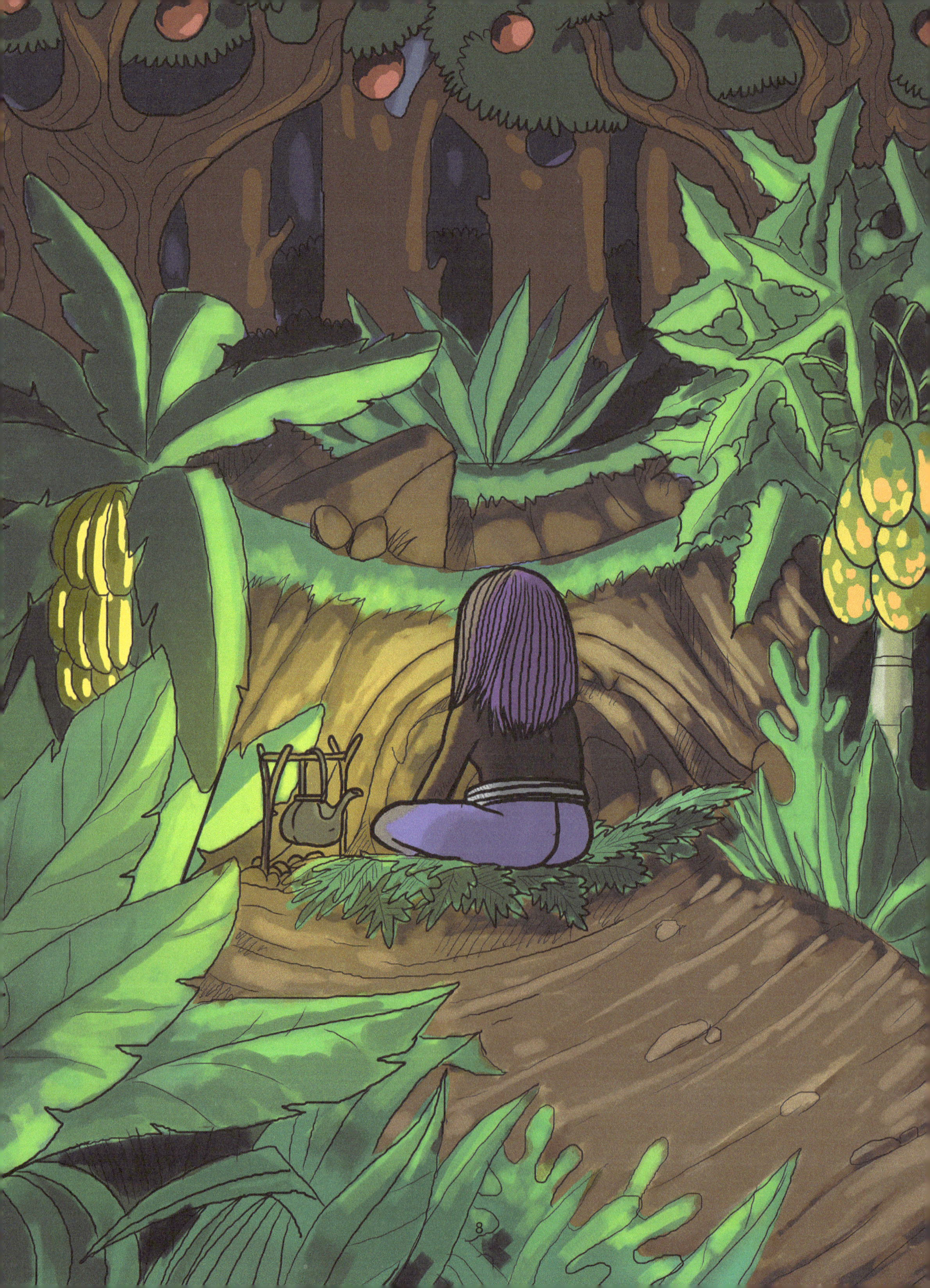

She did not find the chicken by the forest, and the magical space butterfly dropped her off on an island. There was a king who lived the life the vagabond envisioned. His presence radiated warmth, and the little princess called him king of the island.

The King said, "Living on this big island means being dutiful and accepting big responsibilities. The island is large, and I provide jobs for many families who live on it. Everyone is in the same position as I am—with access to schools, hospitals, and roads that I have built with my able and talented men—only without the additional responsibilities expected of a King."

The little princess asked, "You are a fair king, how do you become well prepared in your journey?"

The King responded, "The journey for me is neither exotic food nor a comfortable bed, but the food does taste better when one has a purpose. I sleep better when the work I do is meaningful. I like caring for the well-being of my people and that everyone has equal chance to pursue their hopes and dreams."

We preserve our wonderful culture. We are wonderful, kind, grateful, and appreciative of children who are selfless and honour the hopes and dreams of their grandparents and parents before themselves."

"What cultures are you referring to?" asked the little princess.

"Well, there are different customs in different places. Here, we honour our ancestors with a feast on one particular day of the year. Children prepare meals for their parents on that special day. And families enjoy unity meals with their extended families for the New Year celebrations. If there is a grudge, it is usually forgiven by New Year, and a fresh beginning starts the next day," the King explained.

"I guess the one who's frustrated is the one holding onto the grudge and the one who should let go to make space for forgiveness and a new beginning," the little princess thought out loud.

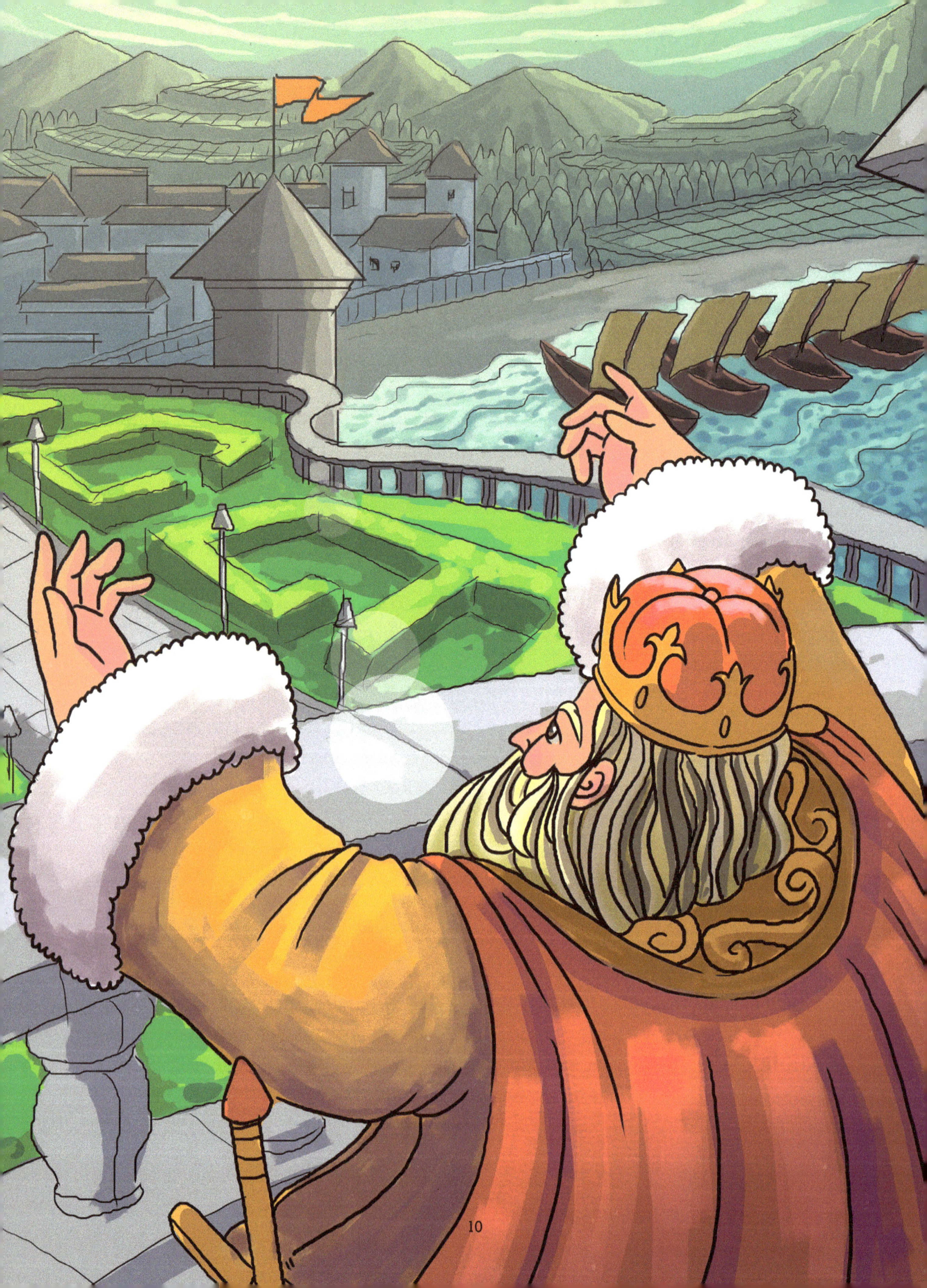

To be thoughtful, one can ask "is it aright, may I, mind if I or what can I do to give support, to alleviate the current pressure you are under? Some things are in our control and others not, and you have to recognise the difference" said the King.

"You are really a special King" said the little princess and she continued "You have the best interest of your people at heart, I hope they realise that".

"I do what matters most to the people," responded the King. "I protect their happiness, their health, and their dignity. When the grand design is functioning as envisioned and producing the desired result—like our clean water system, our safe food system, and our fresh air system—the collective efforts provide the ideal platform. And using this platform, my Children can pursue their hopes and dreams. They balance this with the island's mission, which holds that everyone leaving this island must leave it in a better state than when they first came to nurture it."

"On my journey, I met a vagabond whose desire is your lifestyle, but he is in the woods and alone," said the little princess.

"Well, he has not travelled far enough to access all that has been designed and placed before him. No man on land is ever able to enjoy that which he designed only for himself. Everything is designed with effort for his fellow loved ones. I will let one of your friends have their dreams fulfilled."

The King sent for the vagabond. He was given a team and was provided a parcel of land in the kingdom to rule in the shoes of the king for a period of time to fulfil his vision. The vagabond could not believe his luck, and he started to shape his design. He thought he would be happy when he lived in grandeur.

The vagabond saw the king had to read a lot, was super organised, and had scheduled his busy schedule years in advance.

The King seemed to hold himself to such a high standard. His manners and communication skills were impeccable.

The vagabond's task was to gather a talented team to build his castle. He met a few people with fine craftsmanship and skills, but he found difficulty articulating his style. He had been dreaming of an outcome, but he did not understand what was required to construct pillars and provide structure to his dream.

Soon, the vagabond realised this amazing, once-in-a-lifetime experience didn't fit into his definition of freedom. Now he yearned for his freedom in the forest. While it was not as grand as a kingdom, it was a simple lifestyle that made him happy. The vagabond said, "Now that my dream is about to come true, I see that I didn't realise I would have to work at it. I was hoping it could just be handed to me effortlessly."

The vagabond realised it was not the grandeur he derived happiness from, but his perception—looking forward to what was possible. His happiness came from his love of travelling and socialising through his journey. He also did not want the responsibility the king had. There was no guarantee people would be appreciative or grateful when given fresh water, fresh air, and safe food. And what did being grateful actually mean anyway? Would the people cherish and respect these blessings and care for all they had by not being wasteful? The time it took to build that grand home, not to mention the complexities involved in the project, was too stressful. He preferred not to stay, for if one had not embarked on the journey, one could not understand. It was not the destination that brought joy but, rather, the journey, the process of getting there.

The King said, "When the system is perfect, it is seamless and barely noticeable by the people in the kingdom. People go about their daily lives, which is how it should be. When there is no news, it is good news. Just watch people's reactions. Their smiles symbolise joy and the soul's way of saying indirectly that life is well, and they are at ease."

The vagabond said to the king, "You are one of the good kings. I am happy that you are here to lead the positive way and that you are a man of great accomplishment. I am happy now to be one of those people who go about their daily lives." And he returned to the forest, where he felt sure of himself and his way of life.

Much to his surprise, when he returned to the forest, that was, indeed, quite sufficient. The forest offered plenty of fresh air and plenty of food choices. *Why didn't I notice what I had before?* He wondered.

The vagabond was naturally content, rather than dependent on grandeur to make him content. Perhaps, it's a family unit that would make him content. At present, he also realised he simply enjoyed his carefree walks.

When the vagabond bid farewell to the little princess, he said, "Thank you. Happiness is not far away after all; it is right here where I am. I am grateful for what I already have. Life is simple, and it is my perception that made it more or less so."

By being grateful, he was able to see the beauty and abundance that surrounded him. He saw that he was truly the most carefree person he knew and that he had enjoyed three of his greatest and most valued blessings all along—his health, his freedom, and his happiness.

The little princess did not find the chicken by the island but felt that the people are much indebted to their caring leaders that they'll never know until they perform in the shoes of a leader for one day.

CHAPTER 4

The Little Princess's Fourth Day on Land

On the fourth day, the magical space butterfly dropped her off at a destination far from the island in a city. There she met a teenager who seemed to be deep in thought.

The little princess asked, "Is everything okay?"

The teenager looked up, breaking his train of thought for a moment. The little princess offered support and extended her left hand with palm facing up as if to reach out and said 'I am here, is there anything I can do for you'. They shared a brief conversation before he started telling his life story and explaining that his future was precarious.

"Life's pressures are difficult in the city when one feels insecure—especially for those whose lifestyles are very dependent on their hands and abilities," he told the princess. "With all the inventions, the cows that used to produce milk and feed a whole family are out of jobs in the city. As innovations keep progressing, will I find myself out of work?"

His thoughts about his environment and his society were making him feel a lot of pressure. He felt he couldn't meet all the demands and expectations of him. The more he thought, the more he directed his energy towards these worries. And the more energy he gave the worries, the more he accumulated thoughts of frustration about his situation, which was affecting his well-being.

The little princess wanted to bring the boy to see the King but was mindful not to burden him with every little problem she encountered—as if the King didn't already have enough responsibilities. She hoped there was some way to help the boy deal with the situation and overcome his self-doubt and insecurity.

As the little princess walked just a few metres away from the teenager, she saw a shop with a sign that read, "We are experts. We can coach on all life matters. Come in for a free first consultation."

The little princess walked back to the teenager, encouraging him to broaden his horizon and said, "I saw an alternative option. Why not give something new a try for once? You have nothing to lose."

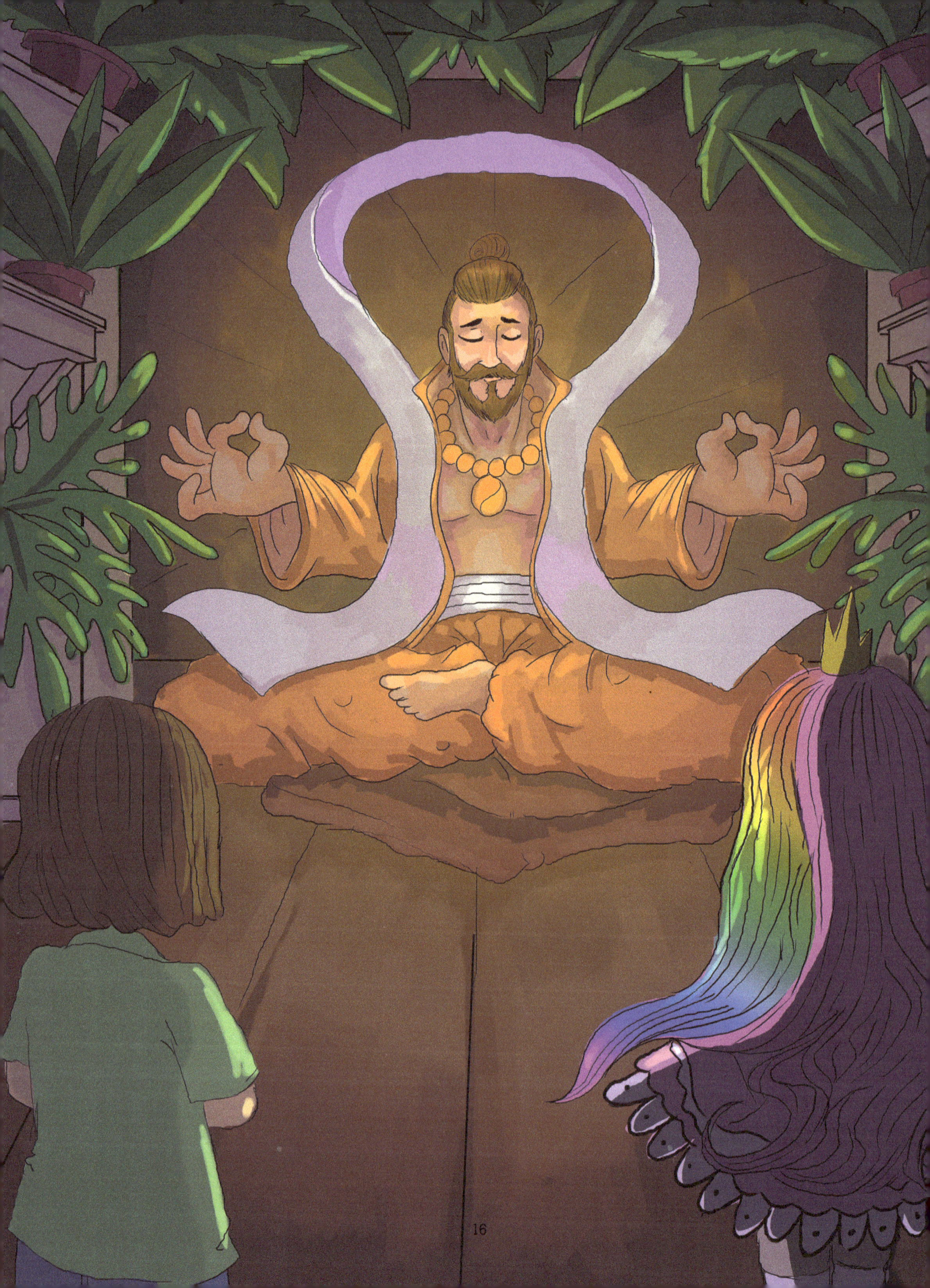

And they visited the life coach.

The life coach asked, "What do you do for a hobby?"

The teenager responded, "I surf."

The life coach responded, "Ah, you get to ride the waves. Very nice. Life is like a series of waves that you have to ride. And like waves, the different situations you face are impermanent."

As they discussed this boy's concerns, the teenager realised he was getting ahead of himself. He was well educated and, therefore, had a complex mind. Because of his complex mind, a lot of uninvited complexities were showing up in his world. To distract himself from the complexities, he constantly bought things, which made him feel good. As so he'd weaved a repeated sequence of behaviour every week for many years, causing him to grow white hair at a tender age instead of natural age.

The life coach said, "Based on your situation, if you simply live within your means, follow a secure saving system that work for you, you will not have to worry about the changing external environment such as changing technology or changing nature of tides".

"I am one of those people who spend more than they earn, so the pay raises I've received over the years have made no difference," said the teenager.

"I used to live with my parents," he continued, "and had no idea about repayment commitments for each choice I make and in entering bigger commitments like buying a new car."

The life coach said, "Normally, if you want to grow your earnings, you improve your capabilities. If you don't want to grow your capabilities, you have fewer wants. You are developing your spending patterns and saving patterns every day. If you let some of the things go, can you continue to surf? Can you still start from the relaxing state of pursuing your hobbies and let it bring you to the end state of joy while still following a system that fits into your habits and comfort level?"

The teenager realised he enjoyed pursuing the fun of surfing. It made his love of life feel alive. But apart from his hobby, many items he was collecting were to build an environment that felt homey. Everything he collected was a bonus to his lifestyle. Seeing that most of these items were not necessities to his livelihood, he wondered, *Are they really more like status symbols?*

The teenager contemplated taking the bus to be part of the compassionate side, instead of the comparison cycle. He tried not to surrender to his friends' opinion and to the pressure to upgrade to the latest gadgets for his collection. He would be patient and would not expand his world to more than he could carry in his suitcase. He realised that, as a teenager, he was more susceptible to peer pressure than he had been when he was a kid. He said, "Being a teenager has its own challenges. Some of us have the tendency to be impulsive, rather than being thoughtful about our tendencies and patterns."

The life coach said, "If you are chasing a sense of belonging, acceptance, and validation from your peers, things have to change. Your sense of self-worth must come from within, and it is you who must refrain from measuring yourself against what you have or don't have in your room.

"It is perfectly valid to want to preserve some personal power to feel secure and, at times, to embrace newness—when you are comfortable to do so".

The teenager felt a sense of direction and understood the underlying cause of his insecurities was being oblivious to his spending habits and his own self-perpetuating patterns—a pattern perpetuated by the fact that the instantaneous gratification felt wonderful every time.

The teenager said, "When I was living with my parents, they told me to save for the rainy day, but it never sunk in. I chose to live a lifestyle that exceeded my means, and the consequence is almost my own self-fulfilling prophecy."

With the life coach's observations, the teenager decided one way to better his situation was to be aware of his lifestyle. He would learn to be humble and grounded and to restore the inner foundation he had when he was living at home with his parents, as well as reassessing his habits and how they had evolved since he moved out of home.

The teenager realised what's changed was he used to be carefree and then growing up learned to accept responsibilities, and these responsibilities included learning new skills, to be able to cook, pack for the next day's task, clean his room without being requested. He believed this to be each person's level of maturity, this responsibility is balanced with choice. He now has the choice to cook his favourite dishes whereas when he was at home, it was any food that were prepared for him. He also realised another factor, bigger toys and said "I didn't need so many big items, I will keep it simple".

The life coach said, "If you learn to manage your temptations, instead, focus more on your attitude—on building discipline, self-constitution, and patience—your relationships, the environment, and the community will also benefit from your growth. The separation from your wants may be a little uncomfortable. However, you will feel the load lighten. You are letting go of the possessions' hold on you. You are also letting go of the ongoing care and future maintenance of the items. You will have more time to call your parents, visit them if they are in a nursing home and bring something they can delight in, play their favourite music, send a postcard."

The teenager realised, "I always look forward to the next purchase because it excites me. I forgot I can look forward to helping my parents mow their lawn, plant more bok choy seeds in their garden. They raised me for the first half of my life, cooked for me daily, put roof on top of my head and cared for me when I was unwell. That's a lot of love, I need to be there for them, I'll be more rational about my spending habits by checking in on my short-term gratification and prioritise what really matters."

The life coach also said, "You know what you are not?"

The teenager silently listened.

"You are not an impulsive person who doesn't know what is important to you. You are sensible enough to know how to make sensible choices that reflect who you are. Go forth and make everyone proud."

The teenager thanked the life coach for the session and said, "Thank you. I've just realised things do not define me. The truer definition are the healthy habits I pickup in my journey, and the values I represent. I am part of the cause as well as the solution to my current situation. Everyone is at different phases of their lives. I am choosing to accept my situation as is without comparison and to see the good in everyone and their journey. It has to start from somewhere, from someone. Let me do my part."

The teenager said, "Life feels less strained when one is aware of the underlying cause." He also thanked the little princess before they went their separate ways.

The little princess found many chickens in the city, but none of them were Sweetie Pinky.

CHAPTER 5

The Little Princess's Fifth Day on Land

On the fifth day, the magical space butterfly dropped her off at another far location—this time on the top of a mountain range. And there lived a philosopher. The philosopher was meditating when the little princess arrived.

She wondered tipping toe and whispered, "Excuse me, what are you doing?"

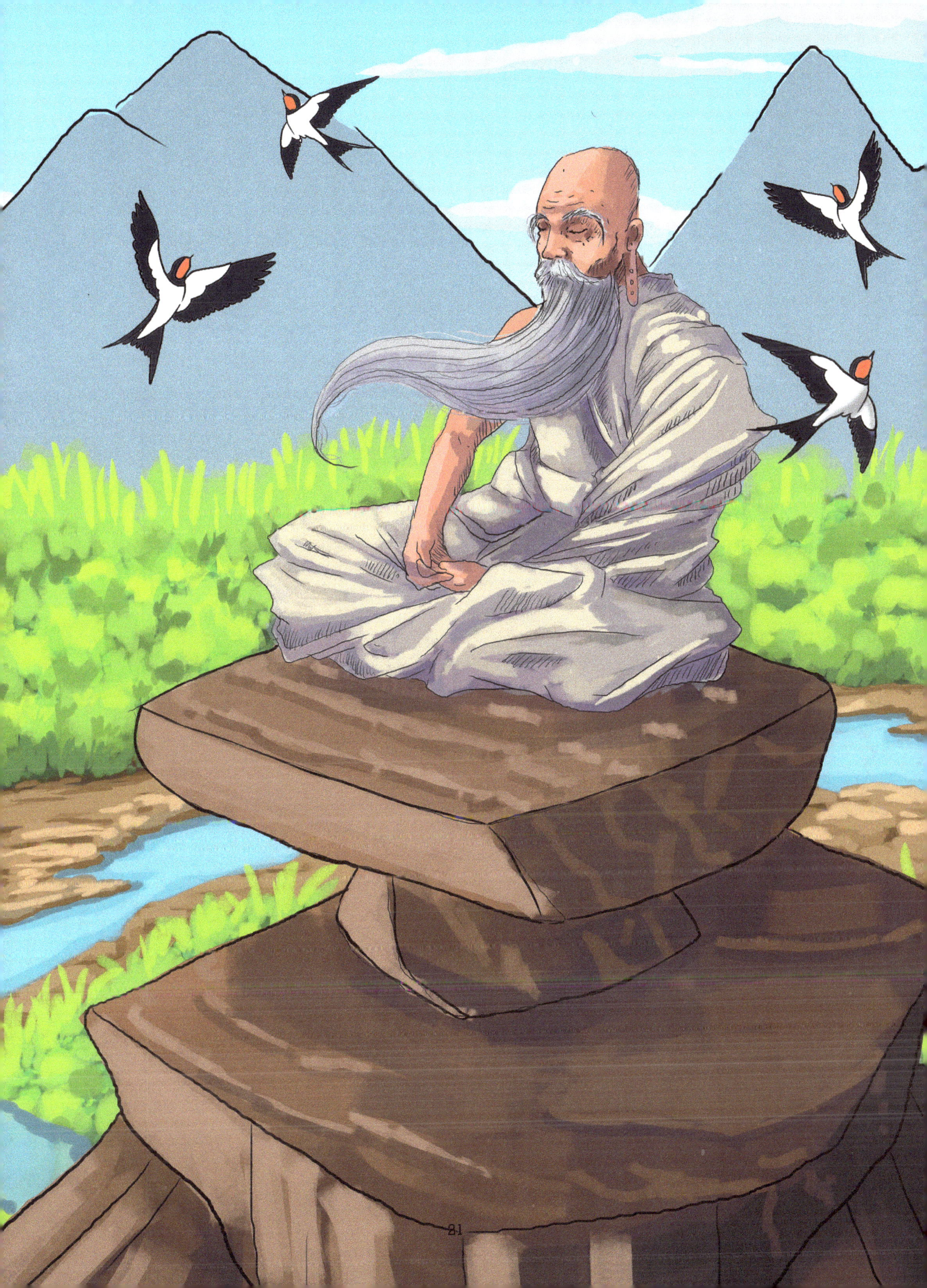

The philosopher smiled calmly and seemed to be radiating serenity from within, "Some would think I am meditating for inner peace. However, I am meditating for the cycle of balance between human and nature to live harmoniously together."

From where the philosopher was sitting, a spectacular view of the four different communities in the north, the east, the west, and the south stretched out before him. The philosopher said, "Nature is perfect. It thrives whether with or without unreasonable interference. If unreasonable interference seeks to beautify nature, then it assists nature, giving it time to replenish and bloom with the seasons. All people are born pure. It is, then, their choices that deliver the world to its current state. Nature reflects back the care and attention put into it. Community reflects back the values and decisions that shape its design. A beautiful environment is not designed overnight but, rather, the result of cumulative collective decisions and communal efforts over time by those who keep care in all they think and do."

The philosopher seemed most simple and had minimal possessions, yet he seemed unnerved by this "lack." He was polite and calm in his demeanour and manners. He wasn't chasing a higher appetite or more comfort. He seemed at ease and in harmony with everything.

The little princess felt very peaceful around the philosopher. The ambience and the mood here was very tranquil as compared to the city lifestyle.

"How come you can sit quietly and be at peace with everything?" asked the little princess.

"I feel my extrinsic values are satisfied. I am seeking to cultivate intrinsic value," replied the philosopher.

"What brings you here?" asked the philosopher.

"I am seeking my Sweetie Pinky," said the little princess.

"What one seeks, one will find," said the philosopher.

"Does everyone have to seek something when they are here?" asked the little princess.

"One need not seek anything when one is fulfilled. One is only here for an extended temporary holiday. Make the most of it with what matters to you. What matters to you is what you seek. What you seek is what you spend most of your time on. What you spend most of your time on is what you value. And what you value is what gives you the experience and memorable moments that matters on this holiday," said the philosopher.

"How can one be fulfilled?" asked the little princess.

"That depends on the individual. One can plant a garden of snapdragon, lilium oriental and peony seeds, and ritually observe it grow will derive a certain level of happiness, satisfaction and fulfillment because of the care and attention given to it. However, that's a question for you to reflect on what it is within your reach, your source of purpose, meaning or enjoyment; whether it will meet your expectations, and if it does, will also make you feel fulfilled. The little princess then shared the teenager's predicament of which the philosopher responded *"Nothing is ever too late for the one who is willing to learn. His current challenges would come to pass with time when he reaches his level of maturity"*.

The little princess would continue to reflect on that question. She thanked the philosopher for his wisdom and continued her journey.

CHAPTER 6

The Little Princess's Sixth Day on Land

On the sixth day, the magical space butterfly dropped her off in another location. Now she was near the ocean. And there lived a little prince.

The little prince was seeking his Rose, while the little princess was seeking her chicken, Sweetie Pinky.

The Little Prince and Rose met as strangers and became friends. Their friendship then bloomed to become something more but the little prince was too naive to understand their mutual feelings not knowing what he now understands. He parted ways without telling Rose he didn't confide in her when she expected upfront communication if something was upsetting him. His sudden departure left an indelible mark of emptiness for both parties. When the little prince returned to where he first met Rose, she was no longer there. This the little prince learned an important lesson to practice his communications and have more courage to communicate so as to never lose something delicate that he'll treasure preciously.

The little prince welcomed the little princess, for he felt he could relate to her predicament and that they shared something in common.

"Are you not curious? Have you tried hamburgers or spaghetti? I have met a 102-year-old man from a village who had never tasted spaghetti his whole life, and his great-granddaughter borrowed a drone to deliver all the ingredients and fulfilled his last request," said the little prince.

"I met a 102-year-old lady who said everything will be all right," said the little princess.

"I was once bitten by a snake who claimed I would return home. But instead, I found myself drifting through the oceans and taken in by a kind king who was very different to another dominant king I'd met prior to the snakebite. The kind king was also very strict with me, as I tend to wonder a lot, and everything was new to me," said the little prince.

"I learned to be on good terms with everyone, including the snake," he added. "But I never allowed myself to get bitten by it again."

He continued. "I also forgave myself for what I didn't understand then as I do now, in order to develop the wisdom to never repeat it. I surrendered to my sorrows then and could not see past my nose. Since my days didn't get washed away just like that, I am cherishing my better days now. I am grateful for today."

The little prince then showed the little princess luxury, a world she never knew and how it took a thousand years to reach its current design. He explained that, where his castle sat used to be plain land. All kinds of unrefined people labelled without hope of healing, recovering, or crossing the line had settled here—without any chance of returning to their homeland. All these unrefined people had then made this place home. Fast-forward over the years, and they had to fight off a rabbit invasion and build a water system. And when households had access to water and electricity, life was comfortable. Then came fine couches, radios, televisions, and mobile phones. Life became exceedingly more comfortable, and some people grew more demanding, more impatient, and more forgetful—no longer grateful for how far they'd come together. Since they are all beneficiaries of all the past sacrifices and contributions, the minimum they can do is reflect on those who made a positive difference and say "thank you".

26

Then the little prince invited the little princess to his space shuttle. "You're the first person I'm taking on this space shuttle," he said.

To the little princess, it was flying like she did with the magical space butterfly but with two big, powerful engines.

The little prince took the little princess to a place called the first-class dining lounge. There was an à la carte menu to order from and finely curated meals and a buffet with all sorts of delicious food that pampered to the taste buds of all who dined there—all prepared by talented gourmet chefs.

The little prince, like an epicure, delighted in his favourite snack, which was steamed taro cake. And the little princess delighted in the apple tart and crème brûlée.

"Tea makes me feel warmer. A delicious meal makes me very happy," said the little prince.

"Me too," said the little princess basking in the sweet aroma, soft textured flavours of the freshly made desserts with fruits tucked inside the creams.

Next to that restaurant was a huge room with clean white robes, towels, and everything else that provided for a five-star experience.

The little princess had met different people, and now she had a different dining experience that had expanded her horizons on quality of service and choices of food for breakfast.

Then the little prince showed her to the national library, which was a great architectural masterpiece. The lift, made of transparent glass, overlooked each level of the library.

"What a fine library," marvelled the little princess.

Then, for lunch, the little prince took out his mobile phone and selected location and restaurant. He selected a restaurant that had Michelin stars and then enjoyed the meal there.

This place must be a land of dreams, thought the little princess.

The little prince said, "The king shared how the people's ancestors moved here from far away a thousand years back. That's when all the so-called unrefined people were put here involuntarily. Now a thousand years forward, they've developed a first-class country with kind, capable, and productive group now helping countless neighbouring lands in distress and alleviating their struggles."

The little princess was impressed with this beautiful place and its high level of cooperation and communal support, high trust, and high ideals.

"I hope you can stay like this for as long as you can and as far as you can, touching people's life in a positive light. Everyone here is thoughtful of others, considerate of others, and friendly. It would be wonderful to settle here," said the little princess.

"I once met a king of the island, and he said to observe people's reaction and notice when they are happy. He said it's their soul speaking indirectly and saying that life is well. This also means you've handled the affairs of your kingdoms well. Under your leadership, everyone seems at ease."

"Happiness is very important to a person's well-being, for stress can cause white hair and make people lose their appetites," said the little prince.

"You know my upbringing is different to yours."

"You turned out well," said the little princess.

"You have great responsibility in protecting the welfare and well-being of your people. If your parents didn't encourage you to read so many books, would you still be as wise, capable and skillful a prince as you are today?" asked the little princess.

"Books keep me company in times of solitude. Books help me understand not to be too reserved or too open-minded. There is always a fine line when it comes to running a kingdom that must be maintained and balanced. Books teach me to recognise sensible balance in making sensible choices," said the little prince.

"I discovered many people go through stages of their journey, and some will cross boundaries to acquire possessions because they believe it will give them assurance of a secure future as if their present moment is lacking. It becomes a habit if one often seeks what one lacks, instead of being grateful for what one already has," said the little princess.

"I say two things I'm grateful for before I wake up in the morning and two things I'm grateful for before I take rest in the evening," said the little prince. "This repositions my focus to be thankful."

"It's all starting to make sense. We are all on this journey together, and there is a lot to be thankful for, like the new foods you've just introduced to me, the new experiences, and the wisdom you've shared," said the little princess.

"In this journey, do what is right. But don't take it too far and strain your relationships or your health, for relationships are enduring, and possessions are replaceable. Possessions are appreciated, as they also serve humanity as a reminder of their creativity—of generations of honing techniques, fine craftsmanship, and experts in design. It takes a lot of effort to design the clothes you wear, to cook the food on the table, and to manufacture the phone in your hand so you can communicate with loved ones. It's time, efforts, and talents that made all this possible, but relationships are enduring," said the little prince

"True, possessions are always less enduring than a meaningful relationship. And they do express creativity, comfort, and social connectivity. It seems the most valuable possession a productive person possesses is their time and talent then?" asked the little princess.

"Potentially, it depends on one's perspective. I remember an old friend who once said that what's essential is often invisible to the eyes. I learned that lesson and no longer look for external signs to express how deep my appreciation is for this kingdom that saved my life and provided me a home, as well as the platform on which to express my creativity, hopes, and dreams. The same privilege is also extended to you. And this platform can liberate and shine your art through your conscientious endeavour. If talent isn't liberated by creating or showing to others, by self-expression and initiative, then the seed of doubt may take its space," said the little prince.

"It is enough just to be a person of value, to hold the door for someone to come through the lift, to lend a pencil to a peer, to plant a flower in your parents' garden, or to even say a kind word like please or thank you—little acts of kindness. It is what makes unity, and being inconsiderate is what further divides differences," said the little prince.

"I miss my chicken," said the little princess.

"Let's find Sweetie Pinky and Rose together first thing tomorrow," said the little prince.

The little princess and little prince sat in silence by the ocean, admiring the orange sunset, surrounded by nearby flowers sprouting and blooming and birds singing and flying above them.

The evening breeze was calm and tranquil. "Isn't it beautiful?" asked the little princess.

"It's such a beautiful moment just to have a friend to socialise with, some truer treasures are friendship," whispered the little prince easing to the beautiful ambience of the atmosphere and fresh air.

CHAPTER 7

The Little Princess's Seventh Day on Land

On the seventh day, the magical space butterfly, the little princess, and the little prince searched for Rose and Sweetie Pinky.

The little prince realised he knew someone who had a magic mirror, and it could show them where Sweetie Pinky and Rose were. The mirror reflected back to them the many friends the little princess had met in her journey and how they had protected Sweetie Pinky from tantrum-throwing cats to aggressive racoons and wild eager beavers. With the help of all these friends, Sweetie Pinky was safe, and everyone was on their way to the little prince's kingdom.

Wow, thought the little princess, *the unity of the world is a push and pull between the lacking and the fulfilled. I am glad to have met many fulfilled friends on my journey.*

"You've met friends who behave under a system that values solidarity. They are honest, and they help each other and their communities. These people help one another, and this is the kind of system we've created and that's appreciated," said the little prince. "Hopefully, the forgetful ones can simply revisit their childhood wonders and reconnect with those activities that bring them joy and not drift too far into unreasonable and unnecessary activities that steal away smiles," said the little prince.

"What can I do to help these few people?" asked the little princess.

The little prince responded, "Perhaps by restoring smiles to those who grew up too fast."

"Do you think we should ask those few people feeling lack to explore a neglected garden that needs water and care. If they care for the garden they walk on and through the time they devote to the garden, the garden will become more valuable and beautiful and, hopefully, remind them that, even if you love a rose plant, it will bloom for you because you gave it time, care, and attention. It will reflect the love you've given it back to you," said the little princess.

"Perhaps it's also that no one on land will stand in the way of the one who has a purpose— a purpose that is both mindfulness and awakening," said the little prince.

"But what of your Rose, the one who is special and different to all other roses in the world," said the little princess.

"I think I have found my Rose" said the little prince, and he felt happy for the first time in a long time.

"Magic mirror, where is Rose?" asked the prince.

"In the castle of an enchanting forest where a beast lives," replied the magic mirror.

"I'll help where I can," said the little princess.

"You know, parting with Rose has been a sweet sorrow. However, it has made my heart grow ever much fonder," said the little prince.

The little prince and the little princess rode on the magic butterfly and when they arrived at the castle passing a well-manicured garden. As they entered the castle, it activated the sound of a lion which awoken a sleeping Beast.

The Beast was not all expected. He demanded a game of chess with the little prince and if he should win, Rose will be set free.

As they were playing chess, footsteps of another beast could be heard from afar. It must be Mrs Beast returning home from her holiday.

Distracted by the noise, the Beast lack of focus made an incorrect move, and "Checkmate" said the little prince.

True to his words, the Beast set Rose free before Mrs Beast's arrival.

After they rescued Rose, they celebrated by sharing yummy cake with everyone in the kind and welcoming kingdom under the stars.

32

The Little Prince said "Bon appétit".

At the celebration, the little princess asked Rose "What's important to you, Rose?"

"Understanding," replied Rose. "I must first understand before I am able to heal. I must first understand before I am to forgive or be resilient or to rise above all that has happened to me. Each day starts afresh—like I am renewed. Why is it that one has to go through such an ordeal to feel deeply grateful and to be cleansed—to restart afresh and not repeat the unhappy path? I don't want to make it a habit to rely on my past to propel me to understand myself better."

"Do you care about what happened in the past?" asked the little princess.

"It's not about whether I care but, rather, whether I've learned anything from the experience. I care because I want to know if there was anything I could have done differently," replied Rose.

"What would you have done differently?" asked the little princess.

"Perhaps let go of the habit of assuming that the little prince didn't care. He did insinuate that he was going to leave, but I refused to accept the reality of the situation. He didn't tell me when he'd come back and that left an indelible mark of uncertainty. It would have made all the difference if only I'd improved my communications back then and talked through matters that were disturbing him. But I didn't find the courage then. I am just glad to see that he is safe and well. And really just his presence and lovely smile are enough for me to keep going," said Rose.

The little prince always went a little extra mile for Rose to make her feel special. And for the first time, she realised that, when she was held captive in the castle with the Beast who was demanding. No one in the castle was free to be themselves. Everyone had to dress, speak, and do tasks his preferred way, and everything had to be well dressed and shiny, including the Rose. She had longed for the days when she was just free to be herself.

When Rose spoke in the castle, the Beast would say, "Silence." And it was almost an unforgiving experience. She was glad to be united with the little prince and have him by her side—supporting, nurturing, and understanding her without interfering with her pace of growth and expressions.

"I would prefer not to have endured the experience. But then it's the experience that has enabled me to see more clearly the kindness, the care, and the thoughtful actions more visibly than if I haven't had that experience," said Rose. "He always makes sure I have adequate food, and that I'm warm and protected from too much sunshine or rain. I realise now that was a lot of thoughtfulness and lot of love.

"In retrospect, I should not have said, 'I don't care. Did I ask you to do that? Nobody asked you to do that,'" Rose concluded.

"Kindness was given without asking, and I didn't understand why I didn't appreciate him then. From now on, I'll will cherish all that he does for me and acknowledge his efforts," said Rose. "It is these little misunderstandings that make us distance ourselves. Equally, it is also the kindness and understanding that unite us."

Sweetie Pinky followed the little princess around at the celebration, it was time to return to Cloud 9.

"Won't you settle here in this kingdom? Everything you'll ever need is here," said the little prince.

"I came to land with one purpose, and that purpose is fulfilled. I am to return home and bring with me all the lovely moments I had on land," said the little princess

"If you find something you love to do, then you shouldn't be seeking further to do something you no longer love to do. I already have a home I love, and if I keep going, I may not find my way home. The boundary is for me to recognise where I am at and whether it has already delivered as expected. I came for Sweetie Pinky, and this journey has led me to more than expected. It has nourished my understanding and enriched my journey with colourful moments and wonderful friendships that will stay with me forever," said the little princess.

"When the stars light up, remember our brief moment shared here in your kingdom," said the little princess.

"I can see you, all of you, for you are part of me, my memory, my growth, my being and becoming," said the little princess.

"I can see you too," said the little prince, "with my friend's magic mirror." His face beamed with happiness and his eyes twinkled. "Will the stars be smiling upon us tonight?"

"When they are smiling, it means I have returned to Cloud 9," said the little princess.

"Do you have any last message?" asked the little prince.

"I'm grateful for today. Life is a beautiful journey to teach us something. When life gets tough, remember to be even more kind to yourself, for most situations are impermanent. And when life is well, I will cherish all the lovely moments. Thank you for being an amazing support and thank you to all the wonderful people who contributed to me and Sweetie Pinky's wonderful adventure on land. We have basked in its delights. Keep up your beautiful *smile*."

And with that the magical space butterfly carried the little princess, along with Sweetie Pinky, and they flew high into the sky.

Clouds formed around Cloud 9 and revealed a message…Of Love…

Love is an eternal blessing.

That loving hearts to loving hearts gladly make.

An acceptance to complement, to grow together and appreciate for any give or take.

Love is also a duty to accept greater responsibilities, to keep care in all that we think and do, and always seek to be understanding.

To anticipate greater strength from oneself to be able to give support, to find courage to converse with kindness and be enlightening.

Love is also an ability to find strength to heal, to replenish love itself by finding time to do more of what you enjoy, to celebrate today and enjoy meaningful quality time, moments and memories together.

Remember, love can also be a fun filled, joyful filled, and patience filled promise to be lovingly forever.

Heavenly, Heavenly, Heavenly.

If you're prepared to accept this love willingly.

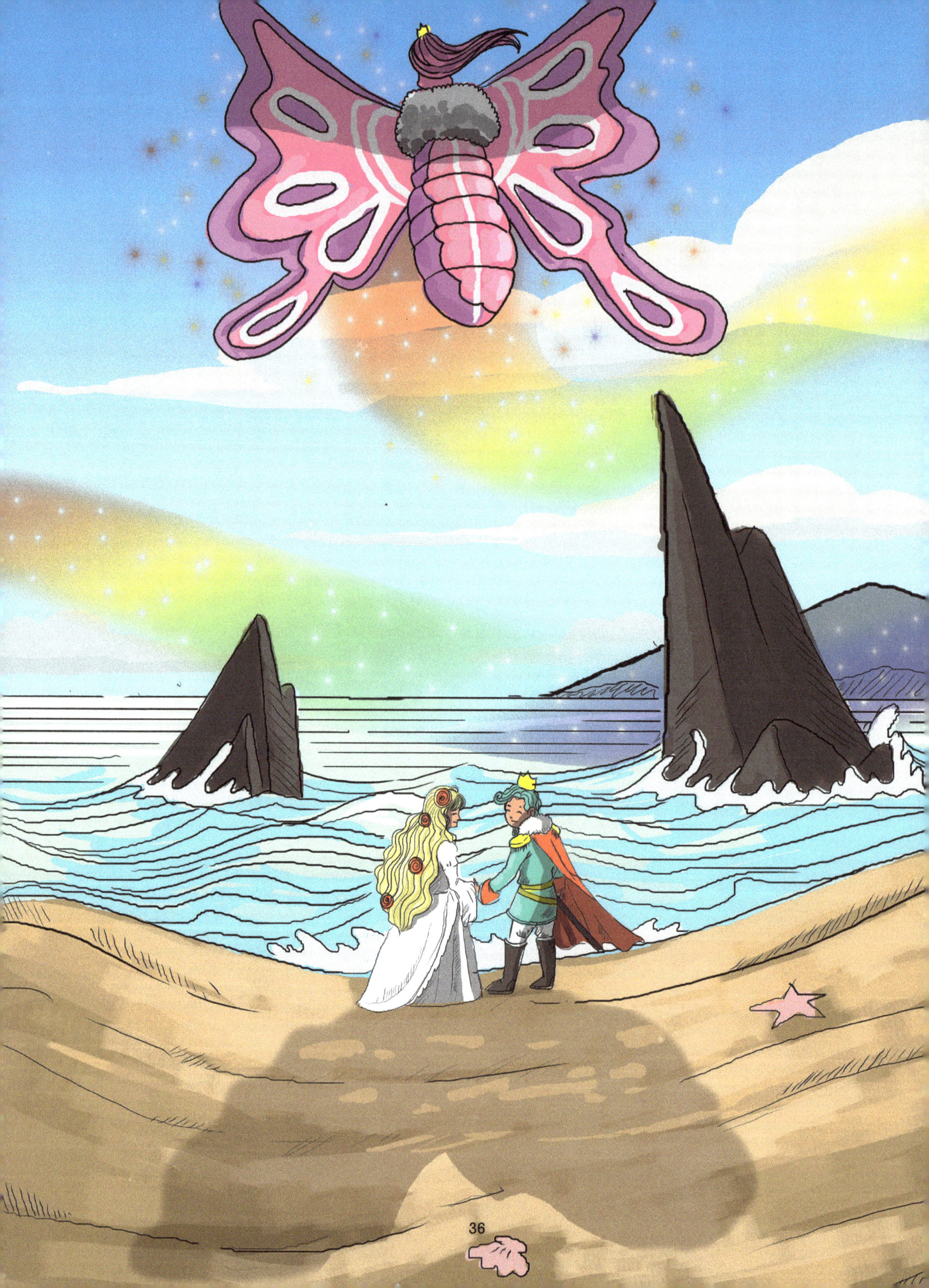